Hi! I'm the bus driver. Listen, I've got to leave for a little while, so can you watch things for me until I get back? Thanks. Oh, and remember:

Don't Let the Pigeon Drive the Bus!

words and pictures by mo willems

HYPERION BOOKS FOR CHILDREN/New York
An Imprint of Disney Book Group

All rights reserved for humans, not pigeons. Published by Hyperion Books for Children, an imprint of Disney Book Group.
No part of this book may be reproduced or transmitted in any form or by any means, without written permission from the
publisher. For information address Hyperion Books for Children, 125 West End Avenue, New York, New York 10023-6387.

Special Edition, April 2013 • 10 9 8 7 6 5 • This book is hand-lettered by Mo Willems, with additional text set in
Helvetica Neue LT Pro and Latino Rumba/Monotype.

FAC-029191-19206 • Printed in Malaysia

Library of Congress Control Number for Hardcover Edition: 2004296657

ISBN 978-1-4231-8370-9

The trade edition of *Don't Let the Pigeon Drive the Bus!*, first published in 2003, was awarded the Caldecott Honor in 2004.

Visit www.hyperionbooksforchildren.com and www.pigeonpresents.com

for cheryl

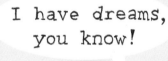